Story by
Barbara Boschen

Illustrations by
Nada Serafimovic

Little Brown Bear daydreamed about pirates and castles and princesses and dragons...well, all sorts of things.

"Adventures...sigh"

More than anything, he dreamed about going on his very OWN adventure but every time he asked Momma Bear if he could go, she always said, "No, Little Brown Bear, you are too small to go on an adventure by yourself."

This always made Little Brown Bear SO sad.

One day, Momma called Little Brown Bear into the kitchen.

"Guess what, Little Brown Bear? You, me, Sister Bear and Brother Bear are ALL going on an adventure in the woods today!"

Little Brown Bear could not believe what he was hearing! He ran to his room to get ready for the big day.

In his room he gathered all the things he needed.

He packed extra socks, a sweater, all his fishing gear, his lucky rock, his other lucky rock, a blanket, a pillow, a snack, a bottle of water, some pencils and paper to record his adventure, binoculars, a compass, a map of the woods, a whistle, a kite to fly when they stopped and a few other things just in case.

When Momma saw all the things
Little Brown Bear was bringing, she smiled a bit
and said, "You are sure bringing a lot of stuff
but I'm worried you won't be able
to keep up and will fall behind..."

Little Brown Bear said, "Oh Momma,
I am only taking what I need – I promise
I won't fall behind."

Momma said, "Okay, but if you fall behind
you might get lost."

And off they all went into the forest with Little Brown Bear following closely behind...for awhile.

They looked at all the nature that surrounded them and saw birds and trees and neat rocks. Little Brown Bear kept up as best he could but his bag was so heavy...he trudged and walked and walked and trudged.

Little by little he fell behind just a bit. He stopped to take the bag off and rest but when he finished and put his bag back on he wondered, where did everyone go? He was sure they weren't that far and must just be up the road a little bit...

He soon realized he could not see Momma, Sister Bear or Brother Bear on the road.

He listened. No, he could not hear them either.

Maybe they were by the river? Little Brown Bear walked down to the river. He was so tired though, he hoped he would find them soon. No one was at the river.

Little Brown Bear was starting to get worried. Were they lost? Oh, poor Momma and Sister Bear and Brother Bear... what could he do?

He decided he HAD to save them but how
would he ever find them?

And then he had a brilliant idea. If he climbed to
the top of the nearby hill he could see in all
directions and then he would be able to see them
and use his whistle to call to them...

Slowly, he climbed up the hill. The backpack felt
like it was full of rocks but he had to save them,
so he leaned forward and climbed and climbed.
Every step put him up the hill
just a little bit further.

Suddenly, he felt the bag shift and before he
knew it he was tumbling back down the hill!

Little Brown Bear landed at the bottom of the hill. He did not get a chance to look for Momma and all his stuff was everywhere.

But something else was wrong. His leg really hurt. In fact, it hurt A LOT. Little Brown Bear was so, so sad.

"Momma", he called and then louder, "MOMMA!" and then even louder, "MOMMA!!" His leg was hurting him very much and he started to cry.

Where was his family? Are they ok? What is wrong with his leg? What can he do?

Just then, Little Brown Bear heard his Momma's voice, "Where are you Little Brown Bear? We can't find you.."

Little Brown Bear called back and soon his Momma, Sister Bear and Brother Bear were by his side. Momma could tell immediately that Little Brown Bear was in trouble and called for help.

Soon the ambulance bears came to take Little Brown Bear to the hospital so they can find out what is wrong with his leg.

At the hospital, Little Brown Bear is examined by
the Doctor. He has broken his leg
and has to get a cast.

As the Doctor finishes putting his cast on, Little Brown Bear starts to feel better.

After all, he has rescued his lost family and is no longer scared and alone.

Sister Bear and Brother Bear write their names
on the cast, which makes Little Brown Bear laugh.

Best of all, while he is sick Momma Bear says
he can eat all the honey &
chocolate ice cream he wants!!!

What a great adventure he has had!

53812889R00018